For Beth Ferry, who helped turn an idea into a story

Copyright © 2021 by Matt Myers

All rights reserved. Published in the United States by Random House Studio,
an imprint of Random House Children's Books, a division of Penguin Random House LLC, New York.

Random House Studio and the colophon are registered trademarks of Penguin Random House LLC.

Visit us on the Web! rhcbooks.com

Educators and librarians, for a variety of teaching tools, visit us at RHTeachersLibrarians.com

Library of Congress Cataloging-in-Publication Data is available upon request.

ISBN 978-0-593-17987-1 (trade) — ISBN 978-0-593-17988-8 (lib. bdg.) —
ISBN 978-0-593-17989-5 (ebook)

MANUFACTURED IN CHINA

10 9 8 7 6 5 4 3 2 1

First Edition

DiNO-GRO

By Matt Myers

RANDOM HOUSE STUDIO ∷ NEW YORK

Cole's newest toy animal wasn't furry, and it didn't squeak. But it was supposed to grow.

"He's so tiny," Cole said.

"He'll grow," Mom said. "You just need to get him wet."

Maybe tomorrow, Cole thought.

Cole showed
Dino-Gro
his tree house.

He taught him how to
jump over the stream.

Wet.

"Don't let him get too big," Dad said.

But Dino-Gro liked growing.

Wet?

Wet?

Wet.

Wet!

"Dino-Gro is getting too big,"
Mom and Dad said.

"What can I do about
it?" Cole asked.

"Don't let him drink
any more," they said.

But Dino-Gro
found the flowers.

He found the
refrigerator.

He found
the shower.

"Dino-Gro is too big to be inside,"
Mom and Dad said.

Cole tried to make
Dino-Gro smaller.
He dried him.

He made him exercise.

He put him on a
liquid-free diet.

Dino-Gro did
get smaller.

But not small enough.

Dino-Gro had
to sleep outside.

Wet.

In the morning, Dino-Gro was gone.

He wasn't
in the yard.

He wasn't in the garage.

He wasn't at
the stream.

He wasn't in the tree house.

"Help!" Cole cried.
"I'm stuck!"

"Call the fire department!"
Dad shouted.

"Call the navy!" Mom yelled.

When help arrived, it was big.
It was blue.

And it was . . .

Dino-Gro stayed big.
And that was just fine.

Soon Cole got a baby sister.

"She's so tiny," Cole said.

"She'll grow," Mom said.